For Laura

Text and illustrations copyright © 2019 by Ged Adamson

All rights reserved. Published in the United States by Schwartz & Wade Books,
an imprint of Random House Children's Books,
a division of Penguin Random House LLC, New York.

Schwartz & Wade Books and the colophon are trademarks of Penguin Random House LLC.

Visit us on the Web! rhcbooks.com

Educators and librarians, for a variety of teaching tools, visit us at RHTeachersLibrarians.com

Library of Congress Cataloging-in-Publication Data is available upon request.
ISBN 978-1-9848-3053-1 (trade) — ISBN 978-1-9848-3054-8 (lib. bdg.) — ISBN 978-1-9848-3055-5 (ebook)

The text of this book is set in Regula Old Face.
The illustrations were rendered in pencil, colored pencil, and watercolor.

MANUFACTURED IN CHINA
1 3 5 7 9 10 8 6 4 2
First Edition

A FOX FOUND A BOX

Ged Adamson

schwartz & wade books · new york

Fox was searching.

Somewhere, under the snow, there was food.
And to find it, he had to dive in.

Again . . .

and again . . .

This didn't look like food.

But what was it?

Nobody seemed to know.
"I think it's a box," said Owl.

There was a stick on top that moved.

There were round things on it that looked interesting.

"What if I just . . . ?"

CLICK!

"The box is singing," chirped the birds.

The animals began to swish their tails,
flap their wings, and move their feet.

It felt nice.

Every day, they would listen to the box.

Sometimes the music made them feel dreamy.

Sometimes it made them feel sort of sad.

Sometimes it made them want to

ROCK OUT!

And every night, the box's
music filled the forest.

Until one morning, the box stopped singing.

The animals poked it.

Fox tried
burying it . . .

and digging it up.

He thought that
maybe the box was
too cold. Fox tried
warming it up.

But nothing would
make the box sing again.

Then something happened.

Fox heard a sound.

It went

drip! drop! drip! drop!

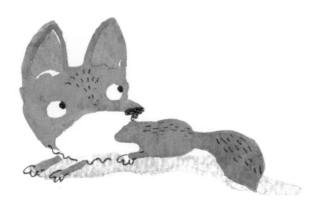

His ears twitched.

His tail swished.

One paw tapped, then the other.

Fox's whole body moved
to the drip-drop beat.

Now the other animals heard the forest, too.

The whoosh-whoosh of the wind.

The chitter-chatter of geese.

The crunch-crunch of snow underfoot.

And the gurgle-gurgle of the river.

They started to notice everything.

The smell of the pine trees, the falling snow . . .

. . . the beautiful view.

And every night, the animals
would nestle down, close their eyes,
and let the forest sing them to sleep.

It felt nice.